THE TREE
THAT'S MEANT TO BE

Dedicated to
the forest

OXFORD
UNIVERSITY PRESS

Great Clarendon Street, Oxford OX2 6DP

Oxford University Press is a department of the University of Oxford.
It furthers the University's objective of excellence in research, scholarship,
and education by publishing worldwide. Oxford is a registered trade mark of
Oxford University Press in the UK and in certain other countries

Text and illustrations copyright © Yuval Zommer 2019

Author photo by Ian Hessenberg

British Library Cataloguing in Publication Data
Data available

ISBN: 978-0-19-276980-0

1 3 5 7 9 10 8 6 4 2

Printed in China

Paper used in the production of this book
is a natural, recyclable product made from wood
grown in sustainable forests. The manufacturing process
conforms to the environmental regulations of the
country of origin.

THE TREE
THAT'S MEANT TO BE

Yuval Zommer

OXFORD
UNIVERSITY PRESS

I
am
the tree
that's meant to be.

I started life as a tiny seed,
but soon enough it was
plain to see that I was never, ever
going to be a perfect, grown-up tree!

I branched a bit to the left,
too much to the right, and
didn't really focus on my height.

While other trees grew
poised and tall,
I lagged behind.

Looking wonky.
Feeling small.

Spring,

summer,

autumn.

Seasons came, stayed, and went.

Then one harsh, cold, winter night,
the forest turned . . .

. . . snowy white.

Then people came with
measuring tapes and saws,

searching for a flawless tree.
A Christmas tree to cut and take indoors!

Soon, one by one,
the other trees were gone.
It was just me, now.

Alone.

I shivered, I shuddered.

'I–i–i–is anyone there?'
I stuttered into the night.

But who would hear my cry?
Who could speak the language of tree?
And understand me?

'Am I the tree that's meant to be?'

And then, at dawn,
a fox,
a deer,
a bird.
They had heard!

Everyone brought
berries, feathers,
nuts, and flowers.

They dressed me for hours
and hours until I was a jolly,
festive tree.

'Hello! Hello!'
'Welcome, squirrel.
Greetings, bear!'
Laughter filled the air.

My clearing rang with
Christmas cheer.

As darkness fell, a falling star dropped down.

It sank into my branches and shone so pure, so bright, that I became a tree of light.

Among the creatures great and small, I felt loved. I felt tall!

Seasons came, stayed, and went.
I am no longer alone,
this is my forest home.

Through wind and rain,
sun and snow, I grow.

Always here,   ever green.

I
am
the tree
that's meant to be.